Squirrel's Acorn

D1613642

Written by Lizbeth Stone
Illustrated by Scott Lewis Broom
Edited by Anne Hartung Spenner

www.bookamoo.com

www.bookamoo.com

We BookaMoo...how about you?

S^{bg}Publishing

To The Ox Cart Man
L.S.

No part of this publication may be reproduced in whole or in part, stored in a retrieval system, or transmitted in any form or by any means, electronic, mechanical, photocopying, recording, or otherwise, without prior written permission of the publisher. For information regarding permission, write to the publisher, StoryBook Genius, at:
4171 Crescent Dr., Ste. 101-A, St. Louis, MO 63129 or visit them on the Internet at www.sbgpublishing.com

ISBN 978-1-941434-13-0
Text copyright© by SBG Publishing 2015.
Illustrations copyright© by SBG Publishing 2015.
All rights reserved. Published by StoryBook Genius, LLC, find us at www.sbgpublishing.com
Printed in the U.S.A.
First StoryBook Genius printing, February 2016
Find all the StoryBook Genius books at www.BookaMoo.com
Contact the publisher at www.sbgpublishing.com

Winter was coming

and it was the season for gathering acorns.

Big acorns

little acorns

perfect acorns

and not-so-perfect acorns.

All of the squirrels were hurriedly gathering as many acorns as they could find.

All but one very calm,
very patient squirrel.

This squirrel
had his eye on
the best acorn
of all...

...the acorn hanging from the
highest branch in the forest.

This squirrel would not compromise on quality.

This squirrel did not want quantity.

Fear didn't change his mind.

Boredom didn't change his plan.

Squirrel pressure didn't keep him from being patient.

This squirrel wanted only the best acorn in the forest.

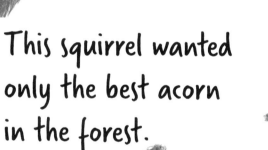

So there he sat, day after day,

waiting for that one special acorn to fall from the tree.

Until, one day...

Squirrel's prized acorn fell from
the tree and landed in his lap.

He proudly carried it home and waited for winter.

Squirrel's friends worried he would not have enough food to last all winter.

They checked on him everyday.

They offered to share.

Squirrel politely said, "No thank you."

The other squirrels soon ate all
the acorns they had gathered.

Every last one of them.

Squirrel was so pleased with his prize acorn
that he made it last...

and last...

and last...

and it kept him
full all winter long.

Until spring arrived and Squirrel
went outside to wait for the next prize.

CPSIA information can be obtained at www.ICGtesting.com
Printed in the USA
LVIW01n0336070416
482407LV00005B/14